Beside the Bay

Beside the Bay

Sheila White Samton

Philomel Books

New York

Published by Philomel Books, a division of The Putnam
Publishing Group, 51 Madison Avenue, New York,
NY 10010. Published simultaneously in Canada
by General Publishing Co. Limited. Printed in
Hong Kong by South China Printing Company.
Designed by Alice Lee Groton

Library of Congress Cataloging-in-Publication Data
Samton, Sheila White. Beside the bay.
Summary: Describes the colorful things seen
on a walk beside the bay. [1. Bays—
Fiction.   2. Stories in rhyme] I. Title.
PZ8.3.S213Be   1987 [E] 86-22562
ISBN 0-399-21420-8
First impression

for Matthew, for Joshua

I walk alone beside the bay,

The water's blue, the sky is gray.

There is no sun or shade at all,

Just white clouds and a white stone wall.

A yellow lizard family

Walks right along the wall with me.

A pink snail in a pink seashell

Walks along with me as well.

And from behind I hear the purr

Of an orange cat, with orange fur.

The stones are set in rows and stacks,

And blackbirds nest between the cracks

Until they fly off on the breeze,

Out to an island of green trees.

Out in the bay the island floats,

Behind the red sails of the boats.

And flying fish, with purple scales,

Flick drops of water from their tails.

How deeply gray the sky has grown!

And we are on this wall alone.

But now I hear my brown dog's bark.

He's come to bring me home by dark.

My walk beside the bay is through.

The sky's still gray, the water blue.

ML